How to Potty Train Your Monster

By **Kelly DiPucchio**

Illustrated by **Mike Moon**

DISNEY · HYPERION BOOKS
NEW YORK

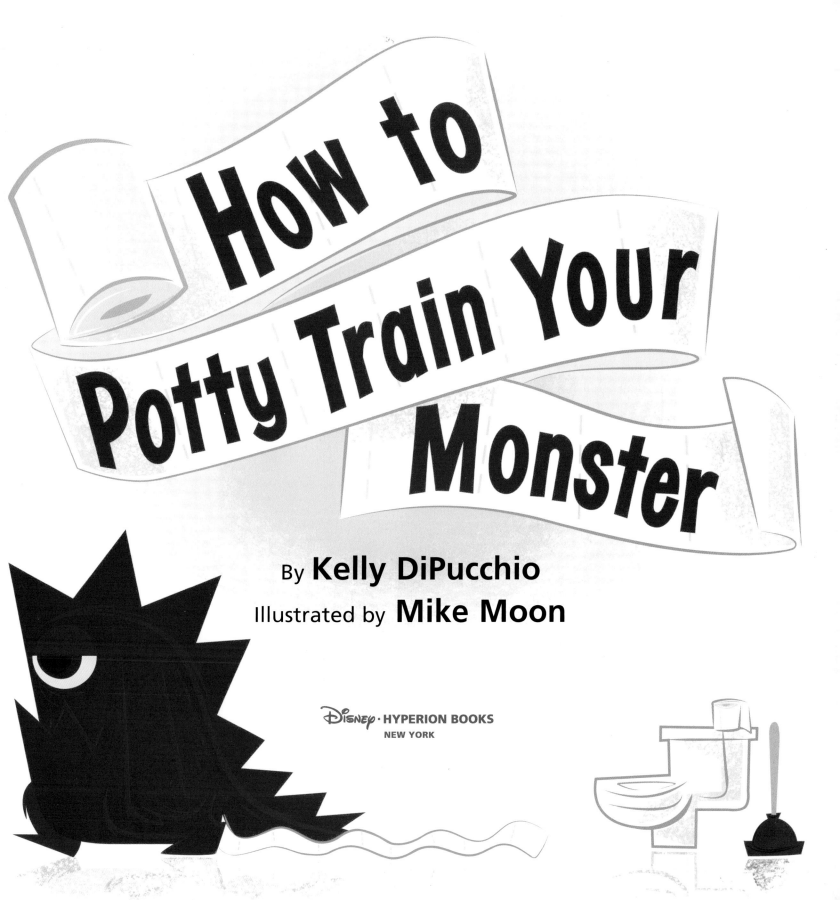

First Edition

3 5 7 9 10 8 6 4 2

F850-6835-5-10134

Printed in Singapore

Reinforced binding

Library of Congress Cataloging-in-Publication Data on file.

ISBN 978-1-4231-0182-6

Visit www.hyperionbooksforchildren.com

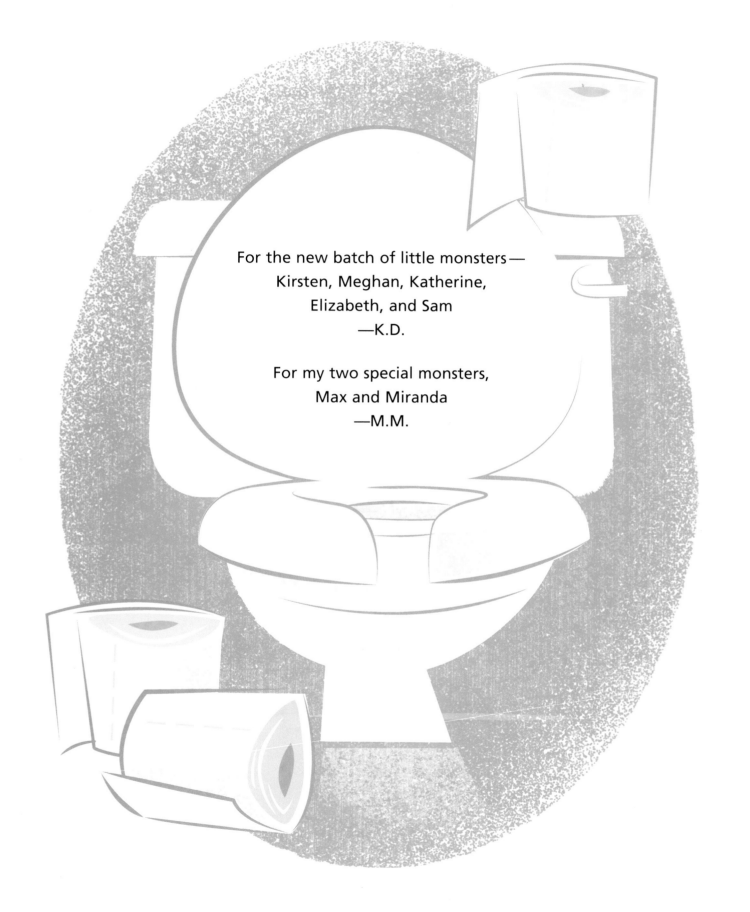

For the new batch of little monsters—
Kirsten, Meghan, Katherine,
Elizabeth, and Sam
—K.D.

For my two special monsters,
Max and Miranda
—M.M.

Congratulations!

Your monster is growing up . . .

. . . and Up . . .

. . . and UP!

He's **TOO BIG** for diapers.

Potty training a monster can be very difficult, dangerous work. But if you follow these ten easy steps, potty training your monster can be a fun and exciting time for the whole family.

STEP 1. MAKE SURE YOUR MONSTER IS READY

7 feet

Most monsters are ready to be potty trained
when they are at least 7 feet tall and between
200 and 300 years old.

STEP 2. GET YOUR MONSTER HIS OWN POTTY CHAIR

Regular toilets are too small for your monster.

He'll need a **great, BIG, GIANT** potty chair to call his own.

STEP 3: DRESS YOUR MONSTER IN COMFORTABLE CLOTHING

Monsters have a hard time undoing buttons and zippers with their sharp claws. Do not dress your monster in fancy clothing while trying to potty train him. Not only will it be hard for him to get undressed . . .

WARNING: Monsters do *not* like wearing tutus.

STEP 4. MAKE FREQUENT TRIPS TO THE BATHROOM

If your monster is like most monsters, he'll probably be having too much fun scaring the neighbors or playing with his pet spider to want to take a potty break. It is important that your monster make regular trips to the bathroom, even if he snarls and stomps and says he doesn't have to "go."

STEP 5: PRAISE YOUR MONSTER

Attaboy, Gloomy!

Monsters love compliments almost as much as they love throwing furniture and eating toenail-chip cookies. After your monster uses the potty, tell him how proud you are by saying things like "Attaboy!" or "Hooray for you!" or "Way to go!"

STEP 6: MAKE SURE YOUR MONSTER WASHES HIS PAWS

It is very important that you teach your monster to wash his paws after using the potty. Monsters love being dirty, so don't be surprised if your monster gets angry and tries to bite the sink.

STEP 7: DON'T LET YOUR MONSTER DRINK TOO MUCH SWAMP WATER BEFORE BED

How to Potty Train Your MONSTER

Monsters do not like to get up during the middle of the night to use the potty. Everyone knows that monsters are very afraid of children hiding under their beds.

STEP 8: BE PATIENT

Give your monster plenty of time on the potty. Monsters have beastly tempers. If he's feeling rushed, he might growl, snort, and throw things . . . like the bathtub.

TIP: DON'T LOSE YOUR HEAD! Stay calm and stand back! Way back.

STEP 9: REMEMBER, ACCIDENTS HAPPEN!

All monsters who are learning how to use the potty have accidents once in a while. Always encourage your monster to keep trying. Say things like "Keep trying, Fuzzball!" or "I believe in you, Lumpy!"

STEP 10: REWARD YOUR MONSTER

You might want to give your monster a small reward each time he uses the potty. Monsters love to be rewarded with stickers, slimy slugs, and dirty socks.

Well, that about covers everything! Good luck, and don't forget to tell your lovable monster one of the BIGGEST, BEST things about being potty trained . . .

MONSTER UNDERWEAR!